Filippa & Friends

THE PIANO

MARIKA MAIJALA JUHA VIRTA

GIBBS SMITH
TO ENRICH AND INSPIRE HUMANKIND

In the middle of the night,
a piano fell from the back
of a truck.

It landed on the street,
rolling downhill with a rumble.

When the piano
finally slowed down
and stopped, it was
in the front yard at
Filippa's house.

The next morning, Filippa was making birdhouses when she saw the piano.

"Come see what I've found," she shouted to her friends André the Donkey and Snoozy the Cat.

"I have always wanted to play one of these!"

André the Donkey was opening his coffee shop.

"Wow," he said. "I could use that as an extra table for those times when I have a lot of customers."

Snoozy the Cat padded up to the piano, yawned . . .

Licorice

Coffee CART

and jumped on top of it
in one giant leap.

Pianola & Son

Snoozy opened the piano lid and jumped in before Filippa even had time to set the piano stool down.

"Don't bother me for at least a few hours, it is my nap time!"

The piano lid closed with a thump.

The day was exactly as André had hoped. It was busy with many customers. So he set up the piano as a table and chair.

"But when can I play the piano?" asked Filippa. She was annoyed, and no one seemed to listen.

The delicious scent of fresh pastries and coffee floated in the air. And new customers hungry for sweets came to André the Donkey's shop.

They admired the piano.

Filippa squinted her eyes as the coffee line grew longer.

Finally, she got upset.

"My goodness, what on earth is this? I found the piano. It is an instrument. I would like to play it, but instead you are turning it into a bedroom for Snoozy the Cat and a coffee shop for André the Donkey."

So Filippa put her harmonica in her back pocket and walked out the gate.

At the same time, the band Gig Time started their rehearsal.

"Where is my piano?" the pianist wondered.

"Have you happened to see my sock?" the conductor asked, searching through his travel chest. "I can't get the beat without it!"

JAZZ-GIG

Friday at 7

"How will I play now?" the pianist lamented.

"Indeed! Try the trumpet," the conductor whooped from behind a pile of stuff.

PICKLED

CUCUMBER

But changing instruments was not so easy. Horns and trumpets just buzzed and rattled out of control in the hands of the pianist. The eardrums and patience of the Gig Time musicians were being tested.

"I think I will take a short break," the pianist finally said out of frustration. "I'm going on a walk."

MARKET - HARBOR

Birds were tweeting in the trees.
Cars were honking. People were chatting.
But the pianist didn't hear a thing.

Suddenly, he was snapped out of his thoughts. He heard someone beautifully playing a harmonica.

FLOWERS

The pianist saw the
harmonica player. It was
Filippa, who was calming her
nerves by playing old tunes. She
had already forgotten all of the fuss.

The little mouse is RUSHING ON,

tHe little masteR is RUNNING along,

lightly padding along tHe gRass . . .

The pianist sat down onto the grass next to Filippa.

"Hello. That's a lovely song. My band has played it as well."

"Which instrument do you play?" Filippa asked in excitement.

"The piano," the pianist sighed. "But it has gone missing."

Filippa thought for a moment.
"Do you know what's funny?
The opposite happened to me.
I found a piano, but I can't play it.
Come with me and you'll see!"

The crowd in the yard had been waiting for Filippa. "Hey, friends, this is a pianist who has lost his piano," Filippa shouted from the gate.

"And here is a piano missing a pianist," whinnied André the Donkey. "It is free now; I even wiped the crumbs off the lid."

"Such a nice place for a nap," Snoozy the Cat yawned as he climbed out of the piano.

The pianist happily rushed to his piano. "This is where you have been!"

The pianist tried to play a few notes, but the piano was silent. "You're not broken, are you?"

"I can guess why!" Snoozy exclaimed. "Open the piano lid."

Filippa did so, and looked inside. "Somebody's sock is in here," she said in surprise.

The pianist clapped his hands. "The conductor will be delighted!"

Filippa and her friends pushed the piano all the way to Gig Time's rehearsal place. The conductor excitedly rushed to meet them. "You found my sock! Marvelous! This will be a memorable rehearsal. Come make music, all of you!"

Finally, Filippa sat down at the piano. "Psst!" the pianist whispered to Filippa. "Let's play the same song you played in the park."

Bum, bum, bum—André the Donkey was playing the bass. The clarinet meowed, the guitars and drums buzzed.

"Bravo, Gig Time!" Filippa exclaimed.

The little mouse is RUSHING ON,
the little master is RUNNING ALONG,
lightly padding along the grass . . .

First published in Finland
Original title: *Piano Karkaa* Copyright © Text
Juha Virta 2015, Text and Illustrations Marika
Maijala 2015, and Etana Editions 2015
Text © 2015 Juha Virta
Text and Illustrations © 2015 Marika Maijala
Graphic Design © 2015 Etana Editions

Published in the United States of America by
Gibbs Smith
P.O. Box 667
Layton, Utah 84041
1.800.835.4993 orders
www.gibbs-smith.com

Published in agreement
with Koja Agency
Text © 2018 Juha Virta
and Marika Maijala
Illustrations © 2018 Marika Maijala
Graphic Design by Etana Editions.

Manufactured in January 2018 in
Hong Kong by Toppan Printing Co.

First Edition
22 21 20 19 18   5 4 3 2 1

Printed and bound in Hong Kong
Gibbs Smith books are printed on either
recycled, 100% post-consumer waste, FSC-
certified papers or on paper produced from
sustainable PEFC-certified forest/controlled
wood source. Learn more at www.pefc.org.

Library of Congress Control
Number: 2017950587
ISBN: 978-1-4236-4926-7

MARKET - HARBOR

Gig Time

CINEMA

SNACKS

TAXI